ANNIE

The Story of a Victorian Mill Girl

Margaret Nash

Illustrated by Kay Dixey

Introduction

During the nineteenth century efforts were made to rescue children from slavery in factories, and to educate them. In Bradford children suffered more than most. John Wood and Richard Oastler worked hard to alter this. They brought the 'Ten Hour movement' to the notice of the nation. Lord Shaftesbury (1801–1885), who was responsible for much reform in factories and in coal mines, succeeded in getting the Ten Hour Bill through parliament.

Titus Salt (1803–1876) built a whole mill village, with baths, school, hospital, church, houses, shops and an institute for recreation. It is called Saltaire.

1833 The Althorp Act – This law forbade children under the age of nine to work in factories, and prevented older children working more than eight hours a day. It also ensured that they got at least two hours of schooling each day.

1847 The Ten Hour Bill – This law was intended to make the working day no longer than ten hours, but this worked out at twelve with meal breaks.

Chapter 1
The Kind Doctor

Annie opened the door and jumped down the steps. Mam liked her to get a bit of fresh air in the evenings, after the mill and school. Throwing back her skipping rope, she skipped past the smelly lavs in the gloomy yard, and into the street.

'Hello there, young Annie.' Dr Leake stopped his horse and waited for her.

'How's the spinning mill these days?'

'Horrible,' said Annie. 'One of the girls crushed her knuckle on a machine yesterday, and Mr Boothroyd didn't care. I wish I worked somewhere better.' The doctor sighed and shook his head.

'Hop onto the cart, I'll give you a lift down the road.'

Annie thanked him. He was always nice to her and Mam. He'd given Mam a job, washing medicine bottles, specially so she could keep the baby with her while she worked.

Dr Leake dropped Annie at the entrance to the big yard, where the other children were playing hopscotch and wheeling hoops, and soon Annie was playing with them.

'Hey, look at him!' yelled one of the girls. Jimmy Spinks was walking across the top of the high wall, waving his arms precariously.

'I bet you girls daren't do this,' he called down.

'*I* dare,' said Annie.

7

'Go on then, let's see you,' said one of
the boys.

Annie began to claw her way up the wall,
using the gas lamp as support.

'Get down! You'll tear your skirt you
barmy ha'p'orth,' said Lizzie.

But Annie was up and gazing at the new woollen mill, out on the edge of town. Six storeys high it was, built by Mr Titus Salt. There was a dining room for the workers, and now he was building streets of houses, with both front doors and back ones, and with their own lavs. How Mam would love to live out there by the moors. But it was not to be. They were only for Mr Salt's workers. She looked at the pall of black smoke hanging over the mills in the centre of the town.

9

'Come on then, get walking,' called
Jimmy Spinks. Annie spread her arms wide.

'Just you watch me!' She took a few
steps, stopped and wobbled. It was scary.

'I can do it,' she told herself. 'I can.'
Then she took a deep breath, balanced, and
almost ran across. And the girls below were
cheering, and clapping.

'Well done, Annie. Well done!'

Chapter 2
A Hard Life

BANG! Annie sat up in bed with a start as old Edith, the Knocker Upper, tapped on the window with her stick. She could hear Mam moving downstairs, and baby George coughing.

'Morning love.' Mam had lit the fire, and already a line of washing steamed in front of it. Annie gulped a mug of tea while Mam braided her hair, and baby George, worn out with coughing, fell asleep in the chair.

Annie joined the others in the dark
street, all hurrying towards the tower of
light at the end of it. Even blacker than the
dark was the thick smoke pouring from
the mill chimney. No one talked. Annie
dreaded the mill and prayed she wouldn't
have an accident, like losing one of her
fingers. She'd heard of a girl who'd had her
whole hand mangled in a machine.

The overlooker, Mr Boothroyd, wore his usual sour expression. He shoved the sweeping brush towards Annie as she walked into the hot, airless room where the machines roared like tortured beasts.

'Clean the floor before you start.'

Annie's heart sank. Sweeping was hard, for the fluff stuck to the oily floor, and the room was long.

When she thought Mr Boothroyd wasn't
looking, she stood against the wall and
rested her aching back. She could scarcely
breathe in the heat. Jimmy Spinks came
past, wheeling his hamper of bobbins.

'Give us one,' whispered Annie. 'I need
a new skipping rope handle.'

He reached down deep into the hamper.
Then suddenly the hamper began to move
down the aisle, and him with it. Annie let
out a squeal of laughter. She slammed her
hand over her mouth. But too late. Mr
Boothroyd was there, cuffing Jimmy's ear.

'Tuppence from both your wages.'

Annie bit her lip. Mam couldn't afford to lose that money. He cracked his strap and flicked it under the nearest machine, just missing her ankle.

'You're wanted over there,' he snarled, and Annie rushed to one of the spinning frames, and crawled underneath it.

Her job was to tie the loose ends of yarn together while the snapping jaws moved dangerously up and down above her.

At last the breakfast bell sounded. Annie's head was pounding as she grabbed her snap tin off the pipes, and went outside. She bumped into Jimmy Spinks.

'Give us some of your bread and dripping.' He snatched at the tin, but she swung it out of reach. 'Come on. I got a clout round the 'ead because of you.'

'I hate Boothroyd,' said Annie. 'I hate this evil place.'

'There's worse places to work,' said
Jimmy. 'Me grandad worked down a mine,
fastened to a coal truck. And me dad
worked as a wool comber till the fumes
from the fires jiggered his lungs. Lads
don't do that since folks like that Lord
Shaftesbury passed laws.' She supposed he
was right.

'Here then.' She broke off some bread.

'Ta.' He stuffed it into his mouth in one
go. Then he felt in his pocket, drew out a
bobbin and gave it to her.

Chapter 3
Keep Awake, Annie

CLUMP! Annie woke up on the floor. Everyone was laughing. Oh no, she'd fallen asleep again in school. She struggled back onto the bench she shared with Lizzie. It was working in the mill from half-past five in the morning that did it.

'Quiet, class,' called Miss Binns. She made them all sit up straight with their hands behind their backs. 'Do keep awake, Annie.' Annie opened her reading book and tried to concentrate. She was thankful when everyone stood up and put their hands together for the last prayer of the day.

'Did you hear about the explosion at Barlow's Mill?' asked Lizzie as they walked down Silk Street.

'I wish our mill would explode and blast Boothroyd out of the window,' said Annie.

'Well never mind,' said Jimmy. 'Empire Day on Monday! No mill, no school and a fair on the common, and my dad says there's to be a brass band competition between two mills.'

20

'Is one of them Salt's mill?' asked Annie. 'I bet his workers will have loads of puff. Dr Leake says Mr Salt built the mill on the edge of the moors so folks could breathe better. He says Mr Salt's going to build lots of things for his workers.' Jimmy shrugged.

'How does he know that?'

'They're both on hospital committees and things. Anyway I know they're friends.'

21

'Wasn't Titus Salt the Mayor a few years ago?' said Lizzie. 'Fancy being Mayor, and wearing posh chains and stuff.'

Annie looked down at her drab grey skirt and sighed. Then she grinned. 'I bet he can't skip as well as I can though,' and she set off skipping down the road, enjoying the new bobbin handle.

Annie took the door key that hung on a
string round her neck, and let herself into
the house. She cut a hunk of bread, and
spread jam on it, then sat on the top
doorstep and thought about Empire Day.
It was always on the Queen's birthday.
She wondered how old Queen Victoria
would be.

Chapter 4
Empire Day

It was a sunny day for the holiday. Annie put on her boots and tied a ribbon in her hair. Mam packed her some parkin, and gave her three whole pennies to spend.

At the corner of Cotton Street Annie saw Jimmy. He was eating a bun.

'You're always scoffing summat,' she said.

'It's m' dinner.' He wiped the crumbs off his face. 'Come on, let's go.'

The common was full of stalls, and everyone was singing the national anthem when they arrived.

'Look, the man pulling teeth has set up near the band so you can't hear folks yelling,' said Jimmy. Annie laughed, and they went to watch the toffee woman pulling skeins of toffee, then to the organ grinder where the children were dancing. But it was too hot to dance for long.

'JIMMY!' Annie grabbed his sleeve, frightened. Men were gathering in the corner of the field. They'd been drinking. She hated people shouting and staggering around. One lurched past her.

'A fair day's wages for a fair day's work! Conditions fit for men, not dogs!'

'Let's go, Jimmy.'

'No. I want to stay and listen.'

'Well, I don't.' She knew he wanted to be an overlooker one day, and boss everyone around like Mr Boothroyd did. She bit her lip as one of the men threw his tin mug in the air.

Annie left Jimmy standing there, and walked through the dirty streets to the canal. It was smelly, but she liked seeing the horses pulling the barges along the towpath.

The canal kept curving and Annie kept walking on to see what was round the next bend. On and on she walked. Suddenly the fancy Salt's mill chimney loomed in the distance. One more bend and there she was, staring at the proud building, its sandstone golden in the afternoon sun, and its big windows letting in lots of light, not like *her* gloomy mill.

Annie walked over to the new houses, which were built but still unoccupied. She remembered Dr Leake telling her how Mr Salt had held a party in his home for over two thousand of his workers, on the day the mill opened. They had all gone by train to his home. Dr Leake had gone too.

She turned round as she heard the sound of hooves. Four beautiful white horses pulling a black carriage swept past. One of the men had a beard, and was wearing a top hat. And on the other side of him sat Dr Leake. Could it be Titus Salt himself? He was very smartly dressed. She watched them ride out of sight.

She started to unwrap Mam's parkin,
then stopped. A flash of bright light
appeared in one of the houses. Was it the
sun on the window? No! It was flickering.
It was flames! FIRE!

Chapter 5
Annie to the Rescue

FIRE! Annie gasped. She must tell someone. But there was no one to tell! She hitched up her skirt and raced up the road, dodging in and out of the cart tracks, until she had to slow down for the stitch in her side. But she was onto a cobbled road, and could see the bright red fire engine further along.

She dashed up to the door and hammered with both fists.

'FIRE! FIRE! HELP!' A fire officer appeared. 'It's the new mill houses,' she gasped.

He pulled the bell. CLANG! CLANG! Men rushed onto the footplate of the fire engine. Annie climbed up too. Then horse and engine headed down the street. The bell was ringing. The horse was going as fast as it could. Folks were staring. Some were following.

Faster, horse, faster, thought Annie. Don't let the lovely house burn down.

A few minutes later they were onto the dirt track. 'At the corner,' shouted Annie. She looked back and saw the handsome carriage again. Dr Leake was leaning out.

'Annie!'

'Doctor!'

Flames were leaping up at the window.
The doctor and his friend were out of their
carriage, and running round the back of
the house. The firemen were unwinding
the hose pipe. As they went in smoke
bellowed out from the house. There was a
loud crack as the window shattered.

Dr Leake reappeared. 'Annie, they say you called the fire engine.' She nodded. 'How come you were here?'

Annie explained. She wiped her hand across her forehead, making a black smudge. The man in the frock coat and top hat was striding towards them.

'That's Mr Titus Salt, Annie,' said the doctor.

35

Mr Salt shook her hand. 'I hear you're the one we have to thank for this fire not being worse. Many thanks.' He turned to Dr Leake. 'I reckon we ought to take this lass home now, John. Up into the carriage, young lady.'

'I've . . . I've got dirty boots,' said Annie.

'No matter,' he replied.

Annie sat beside Mr Salt, and Dr Leake
gave the directions. Wait till she told
Jimmy and Lizzie how Mr Salt had said
'young lady' to her. Then, just as they
turned into Silk Street, she saw Lizzie and
waved. Lizzie stared open-mouthed as the
carriage passed.

The horses stopped at Annie's yard.
Dr Leake helped her down, and said they'd
got to get back. 'You're a credit to your
mam, Annie. Go in and tell her all about
it.' Then he was back in the carriage,
Mr Salt was waving, and they were off.

Chapter 6
Well Done, Annie

Mam was still talking about Annie's
adventure the next morning.

'Was it a grand mill? They say he's got
five other mills in Bradford?'

'He must be rich, Mam.'

'Yes, but he's a good man Annie, in favour of better conditions for everyone. There are some good mill owners, like Robert Owen who built a whole mill village in Lanarkshire, up in Scotland. And our own John Wood and Richard Oastler who've helped get shorter hours.'

'Yes, Mam.' Annie remembered Mam saying a bill had been passed a few years ago forbidding young people to work more than ten hours a day.

'I just wish you worked for someone like them, love.'

Jimmy Spinks didn't know whether to
believe Annie or not. But by the end of
afternoon school he had to, for just before
prayers there was a knock at the classroom
door, and in walked Mr Salt and Dr Leake.
Everyone stared as Mr Salt whispered to
Miss Binns, and she looked at Annie.

'Come to the front Annie.' Annie's heart
was thumping as she walked between the
rows of desks.

Mr Salt told everyone how the sun had shone onto a magnifying glass on the window sill, and set fire to the workman's plans lying there.

'And Annie, sensible girl, got the fire engine and stopped the house burning down.' Everyone clapped and cheered, just like when she'd climbed the wall.

'And now I'll take this clever girl home and meet her mother,' said Mr Salt.

Again Annie found herself in the velvet-seated carriage, and soon they were at the doctor's surgery where Mam was waiting. Mr Salt shook hands with her mother, then turned to Annie.

'Now, lass, how would you like to work in Salt's mill, and live in one of my new houses with your mother? There's a school in the dining room. You can go there in the afternoons, and when you're older you may choose whether to work in the mill full-time if you wish.'

'Oh Mam!' Annie flung her arms around her mother. 'Oh yes, please sir. Oh thank you.' Dr Leake picked up baby George.

'One day all our mills will be better places to work in, Annie, but meanwhile your brother will grow up with good clean air for his lungs, and so will you. Well done, Annie. Well done!'

Glossary

bobbin a wooden cylinder, holding woollen yarn, which fitted on a spindle on the spinning machine; the woollen yarn unwound from the bobbin as it was spun

knocker upper someone who went to all the workers' houses early in the morning, and tapped on the windows with a stick to wake them so they were not late for work; the mill workers had to pay the knocker upper

overlooker a man who was in charge of the machinery, the workers and the quality of work in a particular room in the mill

parkin a moist spicy ginger cake traditionally made in Yorkshire

snap tin a tin used by workers to hold their lunch.